SAVED THE TOWN

by Brenda Seabrooke
Illustrated by Howard M. Burns

Tidewater Publishers
Centreville, Maryland

"Barnaby! Where are you, Barnaby?"

Barnaby peered through the maple leaves. Nobody in St. Michaels could see him perched high in the tree. But Barnaby knew that everybody knew where he was. Barnaby was always up in a tree when his mother called him.

"Barnaby! Come home now!" his mother called again.

Spread out below him Barnaby could see most of the town, all sixty houses. He could see his father's shipyard on the river. He could see his house on Mill Street with his mother standing outside shading her eyes as she searched the nearby trees. Everybody in St. Michaels knew why Barnaby Sharpe climbed trees. He was always telling them why.

"I'm going to be the captain of a ship when I grow up," he'd told Amos Ogleby, the new blacksmith.

"I have to practice on trees so I will be a good climber when I go to sea and have to climb the ship's mast," he'd said to Sarah Jenkins as she carded wool under the shade of an oak tree beside her house.

"A ship's captain has to be able to do everything a sailor can do," he'd explained to Daniel Jones, the cobbler.

Today he was up in the tree for a special reason. He hoped to be the first to spot the British ship and give the alarm as Paul Revere did in the Revolutionary War. But all he could see were the empty inlets and rivers and streams that flowed across the flat land of the Eastern Shore of Maryland into the blue Chesapeake Bay.

"Barnaby, for the last time, come down!"

His mother sounded angry now. Barnaby sighed and climbed down the tree.

"Barnaby, why are you always off in a tree when I need you?" his mother asked when he reached his house.

Barnaby grinned. She always asked that.

"Please fetch me four buckets of water," she said. "Then chop a load of wood. And after that, I want you to mind Peter. I'm making pickles today."

"Can't Susannah watch him?" Barnaby asked.

"No," said his mother. "She's helping me with the pickling."

"But, Ma, the British are coming," Barnaby explained. He didn't want to miss the action.

"I can't help that," she said. "The British have been

coming for over a year since this war started, and we haven't seen a redcoat yet. These cucumbers can't wait for the British. They have to be pickled now before they turn soft."

"Ethan's father said they will burn St. Michaels the way they did Havre de Grace, and Georgetown, and Fredericktown," Barnaby said.

"They haven't burned it yet and we have work to do," said his mother.

Barnaby did as he was told. He didn't mind doing chores for his mother, but he didn't like to watch his little brother.

He couldn't climb trees with Peter around. Peter would try to climb, too, or he would wander off. Minding Peter meant watching him all the time.

Barnaby finished his chores and collected Peter.

"Will the British burn down our house, Barnaby?" Peter asked.

"No, Peter," Barnaby said.

"If they do, will we live like the Indians?"

"No, Peter. Stop worrying. Father and the militia will protect St. Michaels. Let's go to the square," Barnaby suggested to get Peter's attention off burning houses. "Maybe the Blues are drilling." Peter trotted along beside him.

St. Mary's Square was busy. For three days companies of militia had been coming in from all over Talbot County. One company had even come all the way from Caroline County.

They had come to protect St. Michaels from the British who were threatening towns all along the shores of the Chesapeake Bay. Barnaby and Peter identified the militia companies by their badges.

"Look, Barnaby, there's Father." Peter pointed at a group of men.

Barnaby recognized them as owners of other shipyards, Dawson, Haddaway, Wrightson, and Joseph Kemp, who was also captain of the Blues.

"The *Conflict* is still anchored outside Deepwater Point," the captain was saying. "She's a twelve-gun brig and that, gentlemen, is a ship to be reckoned with. I fear for the town. The deserter told General Benson they would attack St. Michaels by land and by sea."

"They won't find it easy. We'll have the log boom stretched across the harbor in less than an hour," John Sharpe said. He broke off when he saw the boys. "Barnaby, take Peter home now. He's too small to be underfoot. He might be trampled by the horses of the Dragoons."

"Are the British coming today?" Barnaby asked with excitement.

"Most likely," said his father. "Go home now and help your mother make ready to leave. We're taking the women and children and animals to Onion Hill."

Barnaby nodded. He could see Onion Hill from his favorite pine tree. It was on the creek behind the town. They would be safely out of reach of cannonballs there.

Then he remembered. "She won't go. She's making pickles."

And she wouldn't go. Not until all the pickles were safely in crocks and stored in the cool, dark cellar to be eaten with meat next winter.

It was late afternoon when she consented to take Peter, Susannah, the cow Buttercup, the laying hens, and Susannah's cat Lucy to the house of a ship's carpenter in Onion Hill. Barnaby helped his father load a cart with food and valuables.

"May I go back with Father?" he asked.

"No, Barnaby. We have to stay here," said his mother.

"But I will miss everything!" Barnaby looked at his father. "Please, Father, let me go with you."

John Sharpe cleared his throat. "Barnaby may be of some use, Elizabeth," he said.

"I want to go, too," Susannah spoke up.

"Me, too," said Peter.

"No," said their father. "You two will have to stay and help your mother with the animals, but Barnaby may come with me."

Barnaby's mother put her hands on his shoulders. "Barnaby, stay close to your father and obey him," she cautioned.

"Yes, M'am." Barnaby was so excited he could hardly stand still as his mother gave him a kiss and smoothed his hair.

"Let's away, then," said Mr. Sharpe.

"I'll tell you all about it," Barnaby promised Susannah and Peter. He waved to his mother and ran after his father.

The square was busier than before as the town prepared for the British attack. Men stood in clusters talking over the noise of horses and dogs. Wagons and carts creaked by laden with possessions. Animals were driven to the safety of Onion Hill.

Barnaby followed his father around as he discussed the defense of the town. At first it was exciting to Barnaby to listen to the men.

"They're after the shipyards," said Impey Dawson.

"And the ships on the stocks," added Captain Kemp. "It's easier to attack an unfinished ship than one armed and under sail."

Barnaby glanced toward the river. The schooner *Surprise* in Sharpe's Shipyard was almost finished. Three other schooners and several barges were being built in the other yards. All were intended for the American Navy.

As the afternoon wore on, Barnaby discovered that waiting for the British to attack could be boring. The air was hot and muggy. Barnaby wished he could slip away and find Joshua and Ethan. But he had promised to stay with his father.

Toward evening Barnaby and his father ate the cold meal his mother had packed for them. It would be dark soon and still the British had not attacked. The sky was threatening rain. When his father met with the other shipowners to discuss the night defense of the town, Barnaby slipped away to a tall oak near the waterfront. He swung himself up on the lowest limb.

It felt good to be stretching himself as he climbed. He had almost reached the top when his father called, "Barnaby Sharpe, come down out of that tree at once."

"But, Father, I want to see the British," Barnaby explained.

"If the British open fire, a cannonball might knock you out of the tree," his father said.

"Oh, no, Father. The British won't aim this high. They'll be aiming lower at the town."

"If they see you," his father warned, "they just might aim at you."

"But they can't see me, Father," said Barnaby. "It's getting dark and I don't have a lantern."

The other men laughed.

"Come down now, Barnaby," his father said firmly.

Barnaby slid down the last few feet of the trunk. He looked up at its branches reaching out like arms. "Maybe if we hung lanterns in the tops of the trees, the British would aim at them and miss the town," he said.

The men laughed again, all but Captain Kemp and John Sharpe. They looked at Barnaby.

"Hmmm," said Captain Kemp. "John, I believe your boy has got something there. It's worth a try. Let's go talk to General Benson."

"Come along, Barnaby," said his father.

Raindrops were falling before they reached the general's headquarters in the square.

"Tell the general your plan, Barnaby," the captain said.

Barnaby felt tongue-tied. He'd never met a general before.

"Well, lad," said the general. "Let's hear it."

Barnaby's father gave him a nod. Barnaby swallowed. "Well, sir, if we hang lanterns in the treetops, maybe the British will shoot at them and miss the town."

It sounded simple to Barnaby when he said it to the general. Maybe it was too simple. Maybe the British were too smart to be tricked so easily.

"Hmmm," said the general.

"The weather will help," Captain Kemp said. "This drizzle has set in for the night. The British won't be able to see very far."

The general turned to the captain. "Do we have a better plan?" he asked.

"No, sir," replied the captain.

"Then we'll do it," said the general. "Go home, lad, and collect every lantern you can find."

Barnaby ran to his empty house. He raced back to the square with the four lanterns that his mother hadn't taken.

All around him people were hurrying to the square, their arms full of lanterns. The militiamen were taking the lanterns to the tall trees around the town.

"Take your lanterns to the oak tree you were in before, Barnaby," Captain Kemp directed.

"Take this rope up with you," his father said. "Then you can pull the lanterns up and light them." He gave Barnaby a steel box with flint inside.

Barnaby put the box in his pocket. He tied the rope around his waist and shinnied up the trunk of the oak. This was the most important tree he had ever climbed. He went all the way to the top. Then his father tied a lantern onto the rope and Barnaby pulled it up. He hung the lantern securely on a branch. Then he removed the glass chimney and turned up the wick. He took out the tinder box and struck the flint against the steel side of the box. A spark flew. The wick caught. Barnaby replaced the chimney. A glow of light surrounded him. Now he was a target for the British.

Barnaby sent the rope back down to his father. While he pulled the next lantern up, he looked down at St. Michaels.

He could just make out the outline of the town in the rainy dusk. Suddenly a light appeared in the top of another tree nearby. And then another.

All around the town men were hanging lanterns in the tops of the trees. Down in his father's shipyard Barnaby could see someone with a lantern climbing the mast of the *Surprise.* Some of the houses had lanterns on their rooftops.

There were no other lights in the town.

Now the British would think the town was in the tops of the trees where the lights were. They would shoot at the lights and their cannonballs would miss the town.

And that is exactly what happened. At four o'clock on the morning of August 10, 1813, the British bombarded St. Michaels.

Barnaby watched with his father as the British overshot the town. In the misty darkness the British thought they were aiming at the lights of the town. Their cannonballs flew harmlessly over the tops of the houses and the shipyards.

Then the British sailed away from St. Michaels. The bombardment was over and the town was saved.

Barnaby and his father went home for breakfast. They were eating hoecake and blackberries when a militiaman knocked on the door. "General Benson wants to see you," he told Barnaby.

Barnaby washed his face and plastered his hair with water so it wouldn't stick out. He knew his mother wouldn't like it if he didn't look neat for the general.

Barnaby could tell that his father was proud of him.

"Barnaby," the general shook his hand. "It was your idea that saved St. Michaels."

"We were lucky," Barnaby began, but the general waved his hand.

"Not important. Only one cannonball hit anything. It went down a chimney on a house on Mulberry Street. Then it came out through the upstairs fireplace and rolled down the stairs alongside Mrs. Merchant and her daughter Jane as they walked down the stairs. But they weren't hurt, only

surprised. Without you and your tree climbing," he allowed himself to smile, "St. Michaels might be in ruins today and all the ships sunk. Your idea saved the town. For that we are most grateful."

Barnaby felt as tall as the trees he climbed. How surprised his mother would be when she found out that he had saved the town. And all because of his tree climbing!

And in St. Michaels, Maryland, as long as people remembered, Barnaby Sharpe was the boy who saved the town.

Barnaby kept on climbing trees until he was old enough to climb masts. He grew up to become the captain of one of his father's ships. He named her after his sister and his wife. Captain Barnaby Sharpe sailed the *Susannah Jane* all over the world.